please, baby, please

by Spike Lee and Tonya Lewis Lee

illustrated by Kadir Nelson

ALADDIN PAPERBACKS

NEW YORK   LONDON   TORONTO   SYDNEY

ALADDIN PAPERBACKS

An imprint of Simon & Schuster Children's Publishing Division

1230 Avenue of the Americas, New York, NY 10020

Text copyright © 2002 by Madstone, Inc.

Illustrations copyright © 2002 by Kadir Nelson

All rights reserved, including the right of reproduction in whole or in part in any form.

ALADDIN PAPERBACKS and colophon are registered trademarks of Simon & Schuster, Inc.

Also available in Simon & Schuster Books For Young Readers hardcover edition.

Designed by Dan Potash

The text of this book was set in Alcoholica.

The illustrations for this book were rendered in oils.

Printed in the United States

First Aladdin Paperbacks edition April 2006

6 8 10 9 7

The Library of Congress has cataloged the hardcover edition as follows:

Lee, Spike.

Please, baby, please / by Spike Lee and Tonya Lewis Lee ; illustrated by Kadir Nelson.

p. cm.

Summary: A toddler's antics keep her mother busy as she tries to feed her,
watch her on the playground, give her a bath, and put her to bed.

ISBN 0-689-83233-8 (hc.)

[1. Toddlers—Fiction. 2. Mother and child—Fiction. 3. Afro-Americans—Fiction.]

I. Lee, Tonya Lewis. II. Nelson, Kadir, ill. III. Title.

PZ7.L514857 Pl 2001 [E]—dc21 99-462286

ISBN-13: 978-0-689-83457-8 (pbk.)

ISBN-10: 0-689-83457-8 (pbk.)

Not on your HEAD,
baby baby baby, please!

Kiss me good night?
Mama, Mama,
Mama, please.

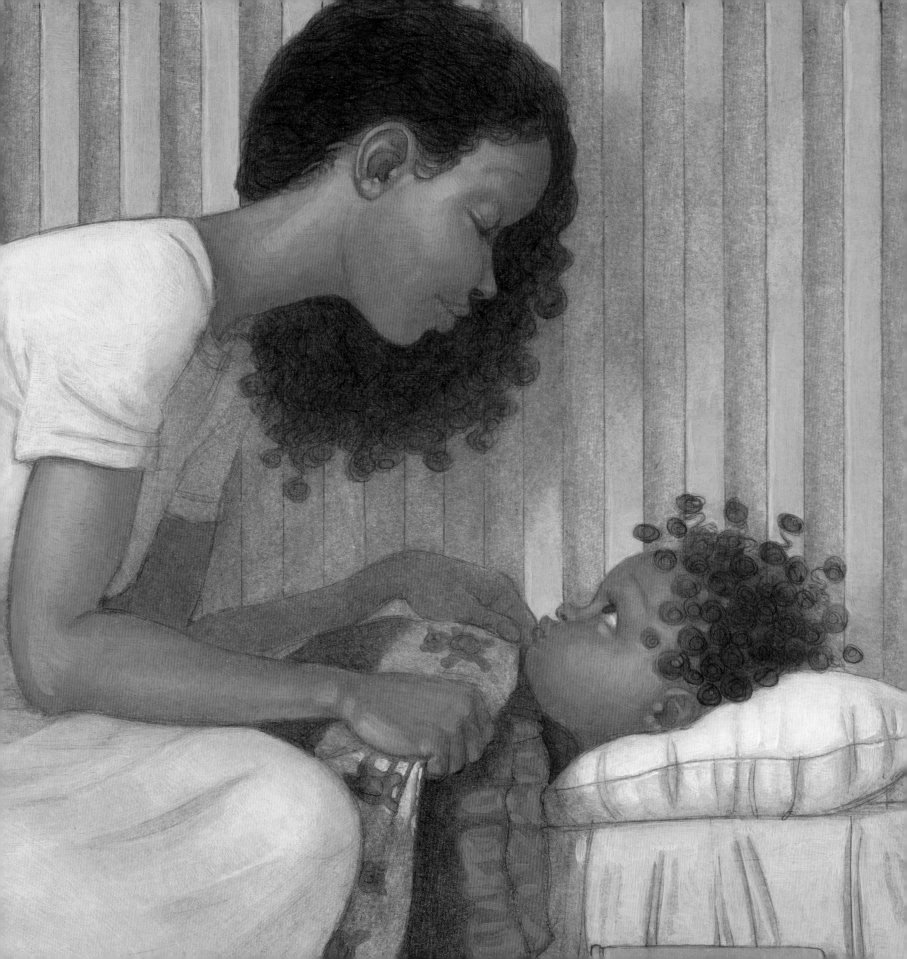

Now you
sleep tight,
please, baby,
please.

O NO! In the trash,
baby baby baby baby!

Please don't splash,
baby baby, please, baby!

Don't be a tease,
baby baby, please, baby.

Please eat your peas,
baby baby
baby baby.

It's time to go, please, baby, please.

Now hold my hand,
baby baby, please, baby.

Don't eat the sand, baby baby baby, please.

please, baby baby baby.

You share that ball,

Keep off the wall, baby baby, please, baby.